THE KINGFISHER BOOK OF
Animal Stories
for the Very Young

Selected and Edited by Sally Grindley

Illustrated by Siobhan Dodds

KINGfISHER

For Jan, a very good friend indeed – S.G.

KINGFISHER
An imprint of Kingfisher Publications Plc
New Penderel House, 283-288 High Holborn
London WC1V 7HZ
www.kingfisherpub.com

The material in this edition was originally published in hardback
by Kingfisher in 1994 in *Animal Stories for the Very Young*
This selection first published in paperback by Kingfisher 1997
as *Crocodile Tears: Animal Stories for the Very Young*
This paperback edition published by Kingfisher 2002
2 4 6 8 10 9 7 5 3 1
1TR/0302/SC/*UDFR/MA128

A CIP catalogue record for this book
is available from the British Library.

ISBN 0 7534 0730 2

Printed in China

Contents

Crocodile Tears

Joyce Dunbar

Two mother crocodiles were basking by the river, their jaws wide open in the sun.

They were very proud crocodiles, because their eggs had successfully hatched, and in each of their mouths was a tiny baby crocodile.

But these mother crocodiles had a problem. It was time for their babies to leave the comfortable pouch in their jaws and join the other baby crocodiles in the swamp, but the babies just wouldn't let go. They were frightened of the big wide world.

The mother crocodiles looked at each other, chewing over their problem. This in itself wasn't easy, for it is very hard to chew anything at all when you have a lot of sharp teeth and a small baby crocodile in your mouth.

"I've never known a baby so clinging," said the first mother crocodile. "He wants me to carry

him everywhere."

"Mine's just the same," said the second mother crocodile. "I've coaxed and cajoled but this baby will *not* be put down. I have to eat on one side of my mouth. Just try *that* when you're trying to tuck into a warthog."

"I know how it is," said the first mother crocodile. "So tiresome."

Then, with their jaws still wide open in the sun, cosily cradling their babies, the mother crocodiles went to sleep.

A crocodile bird came along, pick pick picking at the teeth of the first mother crocodile for bits of food left between the teeth. Her baby didn't like this. They were *his* bits of food. He gave a snap with his baby jaws, but the crocodile bird escaped. It flew to the second mother crocodile's jaws. Pick pick pick it went again.

The second mother's baby also gave a sharp snap with his baby jaws. Again the crocodile bird escaped.

"Yah! Missed!" said the first baby crocodile to the second baby crocodile.

"So did you!" said the second baby crocodile, peeping between his mother's teeth.

"What if I did?" said the first baby crocodile. "My Mum's bigger than yours."

"What if she is bigger?" said the second baby crocodile. "My Mum's scalier than yours."

"What if she is scalier?" said the first baby crocodile. "My Mum can swim faster than yours. She catches more fish."

"Well my Mum caught a shark this morning," said the second baby crocodile. "And she ate it all, and that was just for breakfast."

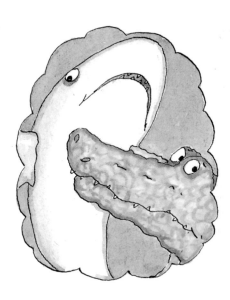

"I don't believe you," said the first baby crocodile. "There aren't any sharks around here. Anyway, my Mum frightened some *people* this morning. Three people in a boat. She frightened them away."

"Did she only frighten them?" said the first baby crocodile. "My Mum *catches* people. She catches them and puts them in the larder."

"No, she doesn't," said the second baby crocodile. "Because my Mum went looking in your Mum's larder yesterday and there weren't any people there. There was

7

only a skinny water rat."

"Oh, did your Mum go looking in my Mum's larder!" said the first baby crocodile. "Well, I'll tell my Mum when she wakes up. My Mum will take a bite out of your Mum."

"Oh, will she!" said the second baby crocodile. "I'd like to see her try. My Mum's got a lot more teeth than your Mum."

"How do you know that?" said the first baby crocodile. "You can't count!"

"Oh, yes I can!" said the second baby crocodile. "Three. A hundred. Seventy-one. Four thousand."

"Well my Mum's teeth are sharper and longer than your Mum's teeth, so there!"

"How do you know that?" said the second baby crocodile. "You can't measure!"

"Just you come along here and take a look!" said the first baby crocodile.

"I will an' all," said the second baby crocodile, "and *you* just come along here and take a look."

"I will an' all," said the first baby crocodile.

By this time, the two baby crocodiles had forgotten all about how frightened they were of the big wide world.

The first baby crocodile slithered out of his mother's jaws and started to make his way to the jaws of the second mother crocodile.

The second baby crocodile slithered out of his mother's jaws and started to make his way to the jaws of the first mother crocodile.

They passed each other on the way.

"Hey, look!" said the first baby crocodile. "We're down on the ground!"

"So we are!" said the second baby crocodile. "On our own four legs!"

They swished their tails and snapped their jaws happily at each other.

"There's the swamp," said the first baby crocodile, "and a whole lot more baby crocodiles. Why don't we go for a splash?"

"We can count teeth later," said the second baby crocodile, belly-crawling along after him.

The crocodile bird saw his chance. Pick pick pick he went on the first mother's teeth, then pick pick pick on the other.

Suddenly, the mothers woke up.

"Where's my baby?" said the first mother crocodile.

"Where's mine?" said the second mother crocodile.

They raced down to the edge of the swamp. There they found the two baby crocodiles, playing and splashing with all the other baby crocodiles.

"Ah! Aren't they sweet?" they said to each other, grinning from eye to eye.

Then they wept, great crocodile tears.

And Fred

Mary Rayner

Fred the donkey stood by the thistles in the corner of his field. It was getting lighter. He was watching for the sun to come up. Any minute now it would show above the line of the downs, and day would be here. Fred took a deep breath. This was his moment. As the first slice of sun slid above the hills, he opened his mouth wide and shouted a welcome, "Heehaw! Heehaw! Heehaw!"

Curled in their beds where they lived next to the stables, the stable lads pulled the blankets over their heads to shut out Fred's brays. Cross words filled the air. "What a racket! Drat that animal!"

And in the big house where the racehorse trainer lived, his wife heaved the duvet over her ears. "Do something about that donkey, can't you?"

"No, I can't," said the trainer. "First, he's not mine, and second, the field he's in isn't mine either."

Fred put his head down and cropped the grass, happy that the day had started well. Bumps and bangs were coming from the stable block, the lads were getting up.

Fred loved watching the string of horses going past his field. Just beyond his gate they had to cross the road to reach the open downs where their gallop began. Fred munched, waiting. Soon he heard the clop of hooves across the yard and along the road, and his great ears came forward as the lead horse, Dark Dancer, came into sight.

Fred took another deep breath, and shouted, donkey-style, "Wotcher!"

Dark Dancer jumped at the sudden noise and the other horses behind him went up on their toes and pranced sideways. The stable lads shouted more cross words as they tried to keep the horses in line. They had just got them calmed down, and were clip-clopping over the road to the start of the gallop, when Fred shouted out again, "Have a good run!"

Dark Dancer's nostrils flared and he chucked his head up and down. He'd have liked to go back and say hello, but his rider made him go on.

Fred watched the racehorses canter off, break into a gallop and disappear over the hill. How fast they were, how graceful! Fred knew that they were special and worth a lot of money. He'd seen their horse box, with the training stable's name

painted on its side and *Horses* written on the back, going past his gate to racecourses all over the country. Dark Dancer had a good chance of winning the big race in a few weeks' time.

Fred put his head down and nosed about among the thistles for fresh grass. He wished he was special. He was just an old donkey in an ordinary field, and the only thing he could do that they couldn't was make a very loud noise. And even that, he thought sadly, didn't seem to please anybody much. He'd never been in a horse box at all, let alone one with a name on the side. And imagine if it said *Donkeys* on the back. People would just laugh. What was so funny about being a donkey?

Later in the day, when the horses came back, Fred didn't even lift his head. He was tired of everyone being cross with him, he wouldn't even say hello. Dark Dancer looked over the gate as he went by, but he saw that the little donkey was in the far corner with his rump towards them and his head down, so he let himself be ridden back to the yard without stopping.

But one night something happened. It was two days before the big race. Everyone at the training stables had gone to bed, and Fred was standing dozing in his thistley corner, when the headlights of a big horse truck blazed across the grass.

Fred woke up. Something was coming into his field. The truck lurched in, did a U-turn and stopped just inside the gate, facing the road. Fred could see its red tail lights. They went out, and the engine stopped. Fred heard men whispering, and the ramp at the back of the truck was let down onto the grass.

Fred stood very still. He was frightened. Were they coming to take him away?

But no, they went out through the gate towards the stables. Fred's long furry ears strained for a sound. He heard more whispers, the creak of a door, and then a long silence. Fred watched the gate. The truck was still there, but in darkness.

Then Fred saw the outline of a horse's back moving along on the far side of the hedge towards it.

"That's funny," he thought, "there isn't any clip-clop of hooves."

Then he saw that it was Dark Dancer, and he was being led into the field. Someone had wrapped something over his eyes.

"How dare they!" thought Fred. "They'll scare him to death. They're stealing him!" And taking a deep breath, he shouted out, "It's all right, Dark Dancer, I'm here. It's Fred!"

But because he was a donkey, it came out "Heehaw! Heehaw! Heehaw!"

Dark Dancer reared up on his hind legs. The rope was yanked out of the man's hand. Cross words filled the air. A light came on in the big house, and another in the stable block. A man ran for the driving cab of the truck. Fred heard a shout, "Let's get out of here!", the ramp was raised, a door slammed and the engine churned. The truck shot out of the gate, swung into the road without any

headlights and roared off into the night.

An alarm bell was ringing, and lights shone out all round the stable yard. Every window in the big house lit up. Fred trotted over to Dark Dancer, who was standing trembling by the gate, and snuffled a welcome. He led him over to the sheltered corner, well out of the beams of light, so that he would not be so afraid.

The blindfold had come off, but Dark Dancer still had pieces of cloth wrapped round his hooves so that they would make no sound when the thieves tried to lead him away. Fred stood beside him and kept him calm.

All night there was coming and going in the stable yard. A police car arrived flashing its blue light, and then two more with sirens going, so that Dark Dancer was frightened all over again. But at last things quietened down, and the two animals dozed off in their dark corner of the field.

When morning came, Fred knew that he still had his usual job to do. He lifted up his head and shouted, "Heehaw! Heehaw! Heehaw!" But this time Dark Dancer had seen it coming, and was not afraid. Fred was a friend.

Fred was amazed to see a stable lad come running across the field.

"Yer little darlin'," he shouted. "There's Dark Dancer safe as houses all the time, an' we thinkin' he'd been spirited away! Shout away, me darlin', that's a lovely

voice you've got, we'll never have another word against it! That sweet music tells us the Dancer's safe. You clever little creature!" And he kissed Fred's furry ears.

Two days later, when Dark Dancer was loaded into the box for the big race, Fred went too, to keep him calm. Dark Dancer won, and when it was time to come home, nobody laughed when the trainer picked up a chalk and added two words underneath the *Horses* sign on the back. A great cheer went up, for he had written *And Fred*.

Zebra
Running

Jenny Koralek

In a land where the sun shines every day there is a beautiful city by the ocean.

The houses are white and pink and yellow. Palm trees grow on the beach and oranges and lemons in all the gardens.

Because the sun shines every day, the children can play out of doors and swim every day. They don't have to wrap up warm to go to the park or the Zoo and the water in the ocean is so warm they can swim in the evenings and then have a picnic on the beach.

The children who live in that lovely city now are never tired of hearing from their grandmothers and their great aunts the story of... the earthquake.

It happened long ago when their grandmothers and great aunts were little girls.

It happened suddenly and has never happened since.

One night, just as everyone had gone to bed, there was a terrible deep rumbling noise underneath the houses and the ground began to tremble and shake. The houses began to move, dishes fell from shelves and doors opened by themselves.

"Earthquake!" shouted the oldest grandfathers and great uncles. "Get everyone out of the houses before they fall down!"

And everyone jumped out of bed and began rushing about, bumping into each other, running out into the dark night and forgetting to put on their shoes.

And the wall of the zebra house at the city's zoo fell down.

Not one of the zebra was hurt, but, of course, they were terrified. Terrified by the rumbling and the shuddering of the very ground they stood on and dazzled by the bright red and orange flames coming from a few small fires which had broken out nearby.

They huddled together and waited for their keeper to come and take care of them. All of them, except...

One. One zebra, who was young and fearless. He wasn't terrified of anything. Not he!

He leapt over the broken wall and away he went. Now was his chance to run like the wind. To run and run! Like the zebra do in Africa when the lion is on the hunt. He had heard about Africa from a flamingo in the Zoo.

So he started running down a street and then another street and yet another, and at each corner he bumped up against more and more

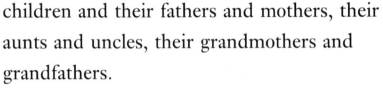

children and their fathers and mothers, their aunts and uncles, their grandmothers and grandfathers.

They were all running too, away from their houses in the pitch dark, trying to find their way to some place where they would be safe from falling houses.

But, just like the zebra in the Zoo, they were terrified, too terrified to think where to go. There were no lights anywhere at all, only the moon, and the moon kept hiding behind the racing clouds.

The zebra ran past them all. He could smell a wonderful smell on the wild windy air . . . a smell he did not know . . . He put his head down and followed his nose.

In the dark, a little girl with very sharp eyes saw the zebra running ahead of them.

Saw his white stripes in the darkness. Saw them shine like
silver every time the wind brushed the clouds off the moon.

"Look! Look!" she called to her brother.

"Look! Look!" he called to their mother and father and all
the other people in that frightened crowd.

"Look at that zebra! Look at that zebra running! He seems
to know where he is going. He will want to find a safe place.
Let's follow him!"

The children and their families followed the zebra as he left
the houses far behind, left the trembling ground and running,

running, running free – suddenly! by luck, or by magic, by hook or by crook, or by zebra, there they all were! Down on the sandy beach by the ocean, far from falling walls and roof-tops and fires and fear. They sat down on the warm sand and rested and laughed and talked and forgot all about the zebra.

The zebra didn't mind. He loved the salty smell and the easy crunch of the sand under his hooves and the swish and swoosh of the ocean's waves thundering on the shore. He ran on and on and on, wondering if this was all a dream and he was in Africa.

His keeper came after him. He had rushed to the zebra house when the earthquake began. He had not even had to count to know that one of the zebra was missing. He knew exactly which one it was – his favourite – the youngest, the friskiest. Off he went, following the crowd, just able to spot the zebra's head above all the people. He kicked off his shoes

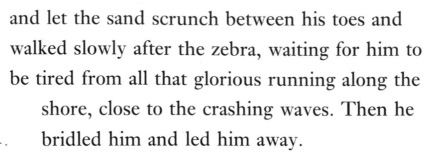

and let the sand scrunch between his toes and walked slowly after the zebra, waiting for him to be tired from all that glorious running along the shore, close to the crashing waves. Then he bridled him and led him away.

"Home again!" he said kindly and then shook himself and said, "What do I mean, 'Home again'? The Zoo is not a home. They should all be running free... in Africa."

And then he had a wonderful idea! The zebra house would have to be mended. It would take a long time because first all the houses that had fallen down in the night would have to be mended.

Next day he went to see the Chief Keeper of the Zoo.

"My brother is a farmer," he said. "And he has a fine field of lush green grass that leads down to a bay surrounded by high cliffs. It would make a safe and peaceful place for my zebra to stay while you build up their walls again."

"I like that idea very much," said the Chief Keeper. "I think it will be a very long time before the zebra house is fixed."

And he smiled at the zebra keeper, as if he too knew what it was like to kick off his shoes and scrunch sand between his toes; as if he too liked the thought of zebra running, running free along the beach close to the crashing waves.

Sometimes, when the zebra keeper went down to that lush green field, he would wander down to the beach with his hand on the neck of that young, lively zebra, the fearless one, the seeker of safety and say: "What a to-do! What a to-do, eh? The night of the earthquake. Where were you running to that terrible night, eh? Running to Africa, were you? Who knows! Who knows! I like to think you saved some lives that night, you, my zebra, as you ran out of the city. All those kids and their mums and dads and aunties and grans and grandpas! Following the light of your white stripes."

Then the keeper would look up at the wheeling gulls and call out to them: "Oi! Pass it on, will you! You know the story! Well, pass it on – this story from a strange and faraway place where zebra are running free beside the ocean. Perhaps the zebra mothers will tell it to their children when the lions are asleep, their bellies full of meat. Pass it on to the cranes flying south, who will tell it to the flamingoes and they will tell it to... the zebra... in Africa!"

Slowly Does It

Robin Ravilious

Something had invaded the forest; something strange and worrying. The Howler Monkey heard it. The Jaguar smelled it. The Macaws saw something moving in the bushes. But no one could tell what it was.

The Something had a strange smell; it left strange tracks; and it made noises that the forest had never heard before. The animals didn't like it at all.

At last, the Jaguar, who was bigger and stronger than the rest, called a meeting to decide what to do. Everyone gathered round nervously. Everyone except the Sloth, that is. He was asleep, as usual, in his tree.

"Well!" growled the Jaguar in his deep fierce voice. "Does anyone know what this Something is?"

"It's much taller than a monkey," said the Howler Monkey.

"It has a shiny yellow head," said a Macaw.

"It makes a terrible snarling noise," said a Marmoset.

"But sometimes it whistles like a bird."

"It smells bad, like fire," said a Snake.

Then the Jaguar asked the question they were most worried about. "What does it *eat*?"

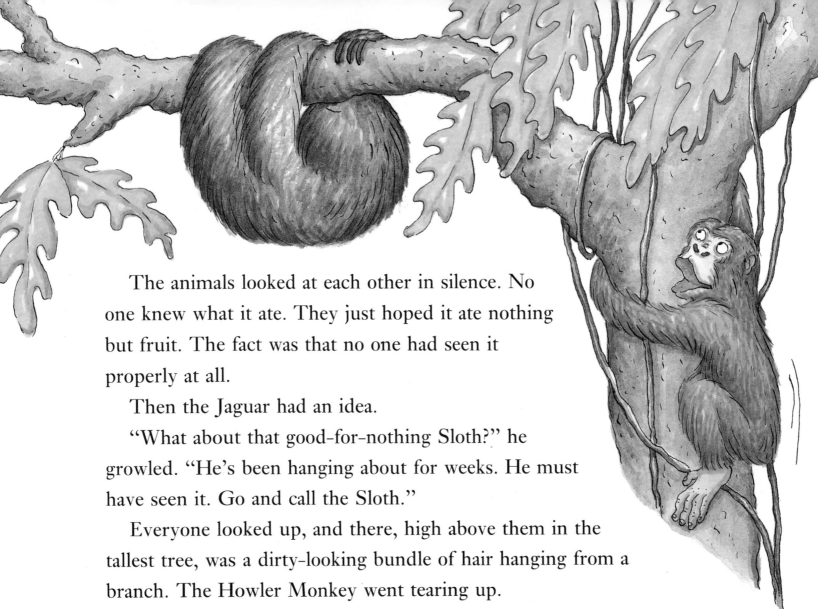

The animals looked at each other in silence. No one knew what it ate. They just hoped it ate nothing but fruit. The fact was that no one had seen it properly at all.

Then the Jaguar had an idea.

"What about that good-for-nothing Sloth?" he growled. "He's been hanging about for weeks. He must have seen it. Go and call the Sloth."

Everyone looked up, and there, high above them in the tallest tree, was a dirty-looking bundle of hair hanging from a branch. The Howler Monkey went tearing up.

"Hey, you! Slowcoach!" he yelled, shaking the Sloth's branch. "Shift your bulk. Jaguar wants a word with you."

The Sloth was hanging peacefully by his long shaggy arms and legs, with his head resting on his shaggy chest. Sometimes he ate the leaves he could reach. Mostly he just hung there fast asleep. He had hung so still for so long that green mould was growing in his hair. He took no notice whatever of the Howler Monkey.

The Howler Monkey shouted and bounced till fruit rained down on the animals below, but the Sloth slept on.

Then all the little Marmosets went scampering up to try waking him. "Quick, quick, quick!" they chattered, jumping from twig to twig like grasshoppers.

The Sloth opened his short-sighted eyes. Then he shut them again.

The Tree Snake went next, coiling and twisting up the tree, and out along the branch.

"I sshould sstop thiss ssnoozing," he whispered in the Sloth's ear. "Better ssafe than ssorry."

The Sloth just opened his mouth in a long, slow-motion yawn.

Then the Macaws had a go. They flew round and round the Sloth, flashing their bright wings and squawking fit to choke.

"Wake up, Slug-a-bed, WAKE UP! Jaguar wants to talk."

The Sloth unhooked one arm and scratched his tummy drowsily.

Then the Jaguar lost his temper. He leapt and clawed his way up the tree, lashing his tail with rage.

"Look here, you mouldy old hammock," he roared. "Are you going to talk, or do I have to make you?"

28

The Sloth peered at his visitor. "Good ... morning,"
he said slowly (although it was afternoon by now). "What...
seems ... to ... be ... the ... trouble?"

All the animals burst out talking at once: growling, yelling,
hissing, chattering and squawking about the Something. The
Sloth just hung there smiling, and slowly blinking his eyes.

The rumpus went on for some time, for the Sloth wasn't
very bright. It took a while to get a new idea into his shaggy
head.

"A ... Something?" he said at last. "What ... sort ... of ..."

"Stop!" interrupted the Howler Monkey. "Listen!"

Everyone went quiet. Up from the ground far beneath them
came a noise more terrifying than anything they had ever heard
before. An ugly, ear-splitting snarling roar it was, and it filled
them with fear. Then there was a loud crack, a huge crash, and
one of the nearby trees just ... fell down. The animals could
not believe their eyes.

"The Something," whispered the Jaguar, with his fur standing on end. "It's eating the trees."

At that, they all fled in panic, tumbling helter-skelter through the branches to get away. In a moment they were all gone. All except the Sloth, of course. He was left hanging there alone, with his mouth open, and his question unanswered.

"Nobody... tells... me... anything," he sighed. "I... s'pose... I'd... better... go... and... see..."

Then, at last, he started to move. Inch by inch he crept along his branch until he reached the main trunk. The awful noise went on and on, but he took no notice. He wrapped his shaggy arms around the tree and began to climb down. Slowly – oh so slowly- he groped his way down, and down... and down. It was growing dark under the trees, and the noise had stopped, but still he toiled on. He was nearly there, and feeling so tired, when into the clearing came... the Something. They stared at each other.

What the Sloth saw was a man. A man

with a chainsaw for cutting down trees. But the Sloth didn't know it was a man. He'd never met one before. He peered at it doubtfully. Then he did what sloths always do to stay out of trouble: he kept quite still and smiled.

But what the man saw, however, in that shadowy forest, far from home, was a horrible hairy hobgoblin leering at him with a spooky grin on its face. It made his blood run cold. He let out a strangled cry, and ran for his life.

Next morning the other animals came anxiously creeping back. They sniffed the air for that frightening smell. They listened for the frightening noise. But all they smelled were sweet forest scents; and all they heard were the friendly forest calls. The Something had gone. And there was the Sloth dangling from his branch in the sunshine, and slowly stuffing leaves into his smile.

After the Storm

Michael Morpurgo

The storm was over and all the frogs and toads came hopping out onto the lawn to play long-jump. The frogs always chose long-jump because frogs jump farther than toads. And, of course, the frogs always won, not that the toads minded all that much. Anything for a quiet life, they thought.

Suddenly, the door of the house opened, and Mut, a shaggy sort of sheepdog, came bounding out, barking at a lorry that was coming up the road past the front gate.

The frogs scattered into the safety of the flowerbeds under the terrace and hid. The toads could not move so fast. So instead, they stayed quite still where they were and just hoped they would neither be trodden on, nor eaten.

Luckily for them, Mut went roaring after the lorry, chasing it all the way along the fence until he was quite sure it would never come back. Then, tail high and wagging, he walked triumphantly over to the terrace and lay down in the shade of the wisteria. Soon he was fast asleep, his head on his paws.

It wasn't long after this that two children came wandering

out onto the lawn. Peter was pulling a small cart. Alice was sitting crosslegged inside and both of them were reading. They were taking turns pulling, but it always seemed to be Peter's turn. Anything for a quiet life, he thought. Sitting in the long grass, the toads did not see them coming till it was too late. There was only time to shout.

"Watch out! Watch out!" croaked the chief toad – he was chief because he was the biggest, and he had the loudest voice. But Peter and Alice heard nothing. They were far too busy reading. It was very lucky for the toads that, just at that moment, Alice finished her book, looked up and saw the toads.

"Look," she said. "Frogs!"

"We're not frogs," croaked the chief toad, quite annoyed;

but no one heard him. Alice and Peter knelt down in the grass and caught them gently one by one in cupped hands and put them in a plastic ice-cream carton. Soon there were so many of them that they were all clambering on each other to get out.

"That's the lot," cried Alice, clapping her hands in delight. "We've got fourteen frogs. Perfect."

"We're not frogs," croaked the chief toad, but they were too busy talking to hear him.

"They're all warty," said Peter, "and they're wet and they're slimy." And he tickled one to make it jump. It didn't, so he tried another. "And they don't jump."

"All frogs jump," said Alice, and she peered into the ice-cream carton.

Now the chief toad was really angry, and he croaked louder than he'd ever croaked before, at the top of his croaky voice. This time they heard him. This time they had to listen.

"How many times do I have to tell you that we're not frogs? And will you please stop poking us? We are toads, and toads don't jump – not if we can help it anyway."

"Well," said Alice, "it's not much fun having frogs that won't jump."

"I tell you what," said the chief toad, thinking as fast as he could. "You put us all back – very gently mind – in our nice muddy ditch down at the bottom of the garden, and I'll tell you where you can find real proper frogs that jump much much better than we ever could."

Of course the children agreed at once and carried them down the garden to their muddy ditch and emptied them out, but carefully, very carefully.

"Thank you kindly," croaked the chief toad. "To tell you the truth, we wouldn't have been very happy in your house. We like it muddy you see, all toads do."

"The frogs," said Alice impatiently. "The jumping frogs. Where are they?"

"Oh yes," croaked the chief toad. "In the flowerbed by the terrace steps. You can't miss them. They'll be jumping." And with a toady smile, he sank into the mud and was gone.

Sure enough, they found the frogs exactly where he'd told them. There were twenty-two of them. Alice counted them, and that was difficult because they kept jumping all over the

place. Catching them wasn't easy either, but at last they were all safe and sound in the plastic ice-cream carton, jumping up and down trying to get out.

"Good jumpers, these," said Peter.

"That's because they're frogs," said Alice. "But if they were kangaroos, they'd jump even better. I wish they were kangaroos!" And just then Granny called out of the window:

"Teatime. Chocolate cake!"

"Chocolate cake!" they cried. "Whoopee!" And they ran. They left behind the ice-cream carton, and the twenty-two

frogs as well. The frogs jumped and jumped, but the sides were too high and they just couldn't manage to jump out, no matter how hard they tried.

Back on the terrace, under the wisteria, Mut began to wake

from his dreams in which he had been burying the bones of a very large lorry. A wasp walked along his nose and buzzed, so he woke up faster. He shook the wasp off and stood up and stretched and yawned. As he lifted his nose, he thought he smelt something he liked. It smelt to him a lot like chocolate cake. He licked his lips and padded down the terrace steps and across the lawn towards the kitchen.

He was just passing the cart when he saw the ice-cream carton – or rather he heard it. He looked inside. Jumping frogs, he thought, interesting. He sniffed at the frogs and

they jumped up at his nose. So he barked at them and then he tried to touch them with his paw, but knocked over the carton instead. The frogs spilled out over the lawn. They never looked back. Away they went, jumping through the long grass in twenty-two different directions. Mut could not make up his mind which one to chase, and so in the end he chased none of them. Cross with himself, he chased the ice-cream carton all over the lawn instead and pounced on it and chewed it and shook it. Then, very pleased with himself, he carried it proudly into the kitchen.

The moment the children saw it they burst into tears.

"Our frogs, he's gone and eaten our jumping frogs!"

"They were our frogs," Alice cried. "We had twenty-two and now he's eaten them all."

"I won't ever talk to Mut again," said Peter, and he pulled the plastic ice-cream carton out of his mouth and pushed him into his basket.

"Me too," said Alice. "We'll none of us ever speak to him

again." And they both cried a lot more and loudly too.

But Granny was looking out of the window.

"I think you'd better come and see," she said, and she pointed. "Over there by the flowerbed." And they looked and they saw.

There were at least twenty-two frogs hopping away happily, all perfectly alive and uneaten.

"Well," said Granny. "Shall we have our chocolate cake now? And I think poor Mut deserves a piece too, don't you? He doesn't look at all happy. Let's make him happy, shall we?" So they made him happy and then sat down at the table for their chocolate cake.

And the children smiled through the last of their tears, just like the summer sun comes out after the storm is over.